# THE TEA

# IS M

# LESBIAN PET

# BY

# ALICIA CASTELLE



## TEACHER IS MY LESBIAN PET

# TABLE OF CONTENTS

# COPYRIGHT

# CHAPTER ONE

Two things were true about Mrs Brown. She was undoubtedly one of the most dedicated professors on campus. And she had a tendency to fantasize about female students, much to her own dismay.

She'd proudly admit to the first. The second? She'd never tell another soul. Ever.

Her life took a striking turn mid-semester after a European History 205 class. She shut off the slide projector and brought the classroom lights back up, delivering parting words along with a reminder of next week's homework assignment.

It was the usual routine whenever class ended. She hung around by her desk while the 50-odd students headed towards the door. Some said 'bye' to her. A few would ask questions. Most went about their day, walking or hurrying away, depending on how the lecture went.

The crowd disappeared, however Mary Peters hung around.

"Professor Brown," Mary said, adjusting the bag around her shoulder with her school supplies in it. "Loved the lecture."

Mrs Brown gave a brief smile. She'd heard it all. While she appreciated every comment about her teaching style, the praise had become banal after doing this for nearly 15 years.

"Thanks. There's more next week. And plenty more after that."

Mary nodded. "Which is exactly what I wanted to talk to you about. Here, I have something for you."

The student reached in her bag and handed the teacher a flyer.

"What's this?" Mrs Brown asked.

"An invitation. I'm a member of the Art Club. We're holding an exhibit on Wednesday the 30th, at 6 pm. I'd like you to come."

The professor glanced at the invitation again. "Well thank you. I should be free that night. I'd love to come."

"Great. But there's something else I wanted to ask you. You seem like an expert on European artwork. Maybe expert is not the right word, but you know a lot about it."

"Oh, there are plenty of other professors on campus more qualified to discuss artwork from this time period. I can refer you to them if you'd like."

"Actually, I'd be more comfortable asking you this," Mary said.

"Oh, okay."

"Because, well, you're a woman. Sounds weird now, but you'll totally get it once you see what I'm talking about."

A stirring comment. Mrs Brown wondered what this was about. What gender had to do with anything. And why Mary was nearly blushing.

"Understood. What's your question?" the professor asked.

"Would you come see my artwork? I'd love to get your feedback before the exhibit. I think you have great insight."

"And where would this take place?"

"On campus," Mary replied. "In the art building. We have a place where we can work and store our projects."

"That sounds doable. But I still don't understand why you'd want me. Professor Keating is a genius when it comes to early European style..."

Mary blushed hard and cut the professor off. "I think it's better if I showed you. Are you free Monday around 10 or 11?"

# CHAPTER TWO

"I can be there around 11:30 after my morning class ends. I'd enjoy seeing what you and the other art students are up to."

Mary's blushing morphed in a light smile. "I will see you then Professor Brown. Have a good weekend."

"You too, Mary."

***

As soon as her student had departed, Mrs Brown returned to her office and opened the university's main website on her laptop. It only took a moment to locate the section for the Art Club. In addition to the list of members and pictures of student-created art, there was also a link to the club's Facebook page.

She followed the link and browsed through the posted photos. On one of them, she saw that Mary had left a comment. Clicking on her student's name, Mrs Brown sat back in awe when the personal page loaded. Mary was a natural beauty, whether she dressed casually or was dolled up. But she was even more stunning with her long hair curled around her face in the profile picture. It reminded Mrs Brown of the sun on a summer day.

There was a photo album titled 'Art,' which Mrs Brown clicked on. Among sculptures and other mediums were several nude paintings which seemed to have been made in the Life Art class on campus. All of the images were nicely done, not to mention stirring.

Mrs Brown gulped. Was this the reason Mary had insisted on a female professor seeing her work? But why did she want her specifically?

***

The weekend moved fast with preparing the upcoming lesson plans and visiting with a few close friends. It was Monday morning before she'd realized it. When her class finished, Mrs Brown headed over to the second-floor studio of the Creative Arts building, where she found Mary and another student working on their projects for the upcoming exhibition.

Mrs Brown greeted both students and asked them about their pieces. The brown-haired boy's abstract sculpture of two birds in flight was impressive. As was Mary's painting of a sunset over the ocean that looked like the water was on fire. Mrs Brown commended them both for their efforts. It wasn't until the boy said he had to get to his next class that she realized why Mary had requested this particular time. It was just the two of them now.

"Here's what I wanted to show you," Mary said, heading over to a private compartment to pull out a canvas and lay it on the table.

The painting showed a strong degree of technical skill in the lines and colors used. It was of a reclined, naked body from the shoulders to the waist with the woman's arms posed behind her.

It reminded Mrs Brown of the artwork photos she'd seen on Mary's Facebook page. Could this be another self-portrait?

While possibly not the intended focal point of the piece, her eyes were drawn to the subject's breasts. They were small and pert with dainty pink nipples. She found arousal spiking within the longer she studied at them, hoping they were in fact a representation of the artist's.

Mary continued, "I'm thinking of including this in the exhibit."

"Why wouldn't you? It's absolutely gorgeous. Consider me impressed."

"Thanks, but does it look historical enough? I'd like all of my entries to represent different periods of European art. I'm not so sure that this one would fit in the post-modern era."

Mrs Brown pondered the question. "As a teacher, I probably shouldn't be saying this, but I don't think anyone is going to debate if it represents the correct time period. I wouldn't worry about it."

"It matters to me," Mary frowned, a rare look from her.

What a meticulous student, Mrs Brown thought. She respected that. You don't see too much of that these days, especially when it came to the intricacies of centuries-old art.

So, the professor took a closer look at the nude portrait and gave a quick rundown of how it could be better suited to fit that particular time period. All the while, Mary listened attentively and hung on every word.

"That's about all I've got," Professor Brown concluded. "But that's just the basics. Like I said, if you want real expertise on art, you should try asking Professor Keating. But, I can see why you didn't."

"Yeah, it would be weird to randomly show a male professor a portrait of my naked breasts. He'd think I was seducing him or something."

Mrs Brown felt her eyebrows rise at the possible inadvertent admission.

Mary must have noticed because she said, "Oh, so it wasn't obvious that I'm the model in that piece?"

"I had my suspicions. The hair in the painting matches yours. So does the shape of the shoulders. As for the rest, well, I wouldn't have known."

Mary blushed. "You're right. There's no way you could have known the shape of my small boobs or the color of my nipples."

Despite the blush on her cheeks, there was a playfulness in Mary's voice that suggested she wasn't at all bashful about this topic, and that made Mrs Brown feel uncomfortable in the best way possible.

The same spark of arousal Mrs Brown had felt while looking at the photos on Mary's Facebook page returned. She suppressed a moan, forcing her lips to remain closed, although she wanted to lick them.

"I really should be going," the teacher said. "I need to grab lunch before my afternoon class, and I'm sure you'd like to finish."

"Oh, okay. I hope I didn't scare you off. It's just, I didn't think you'd mind since you show nude artwork all the time in class."

"I'm not easily scared away by nudity."

"But?"

She gave her student a curt smile. "Lunch."

The light in Mary's eyes dimmed, and her lips pressed together. "Okay, got it."

Mary naturally had an expressive face, and she didn't bother to hide her disappointment.

"You're talented," Mrs Brown added to ease the blow. "You really are. Keep up the good work. I'd love to attend the exhibition."

A hint of that smile returned when Mary nodded. "Thanks Professor Brown. You're the best."

Mrs Brown had a wealth of experience with students after teaching for so long. She was crafty enough to deal with pretty much anything that came her way. But this? A beautiful, young student who had shown her a nude portrait? How could she even begin to tackle it? Or come to terms with the longing she felt inside?

Every moral and professional fiber in Mrs Brown's body told her to walk away and go have lunch. She had done her part. She had given advice. And she had been beyond supportive. Yet, it couldn't end like this.

# CHAPTER THREE

Mary was a sweetheart and her feelings were hurt. There was no way any respectable teacher could leave a student feeling rejected after having bared herself. Both literally and figuratively.

At least that was how Mrs Brown tried to justify her change of mind.

"You look a little tired," Mrs Brown noted. "A lot of students have that look around finals. Care to join me for lunch? I'm buying."

"I can't. I really need to finish up."

"You eat lunch, don't you?"

Mary's eyes brightened. "Fine, but only if I get to pick the spot."

"What do you mean?"

"You buy lunch. I'll take us to a nice place on campus where we can eat. It's a fair trade if you ask me."

"Sounds like a deal," the professor replied. "This place better be worth it."

"Wait and see. Wait and see."

***

After Mary put her stuff away, they went down to the cafeteria and grabbed some chicken and pesto sandwiches along with drinks. Mary led the way up the stairs of the student services building to the rooftop.

There were seats up there that allowed a pretty view of the buildings and trees on campus. To their luck, no one else was around.

"You weren't kidding about this spot," Mrs Brown said, unwrapping her food.

"I like to joke about a lot of things, but not this."

They ate, enjoyed the scenery of the campus, and talked briefly about themselves to get to know each other a little better.

Normally such pleasantries would have made for a wonderful meal, giving a peaceful feeling to Mrs Brown as she got to know a student on a deeper level.

Not this time. A question lingered. No matter how hard she tried to push it away- no matter what they talked about- Mrs Brown's thoughts yearned to remain on the old subject.

"I'm still amazed by your painting," she said, swirling back to the nude portrait without trying to be so blatant about it. "You're superbly talented."

"Amazed by my talent? Or my tits?"

There was a light-heartedness to Mary's tone and Professor Brown couldn't help but look like a deer in headlights.

"Was I that obvious?" the professor admitted, trying not to be embarrassed by it.

Mary nodded with a mouth full of food. "Honestly, I'm used to guys checking out my little package wherever I go. Sometimes girls check me out, too. So I know how to spot it. I just never thought a female professor would be looking at me like that."

"I wasn't checking you out. I was surprised that a student would show me something like that."

"But you liked what you saw," Mary said with a gleam in her eyes.

Mrs Brown tensed. "Mary, I like you, but this is a totally inappropriate conversation to have. I'm sorry, but I can't let you accuse me of..."

"Whoa! Let's take a step back here. I'm not offended at all. If anything, I thought it was actually kind of flattering. Really, I'm cool with it."

Mrs Brown thought maybe she'd completely destroyed the pleasant vibes they'd created over lunch. But Mary's smile seemed enough to smooth things over. It was a smile which read, 'It's okay, I know.'

"I apologize," Mrs Brown said. "Let's take a step back and start over. It's a beautiful day and we were having such a great time."

"I'm still having a great time. But I don't want to change the subject. Your eyes lingered over the portrait I made of my boobs. Big deal. I won't tell anyone, I swear. Discretion is a strong quality of mine."

"You're unstoppable."

Mary smiled wider. "Another personal attribute I have."

The situation was getting out of hand and Mrs Brown briefly plotted her counter-attack. She was an expert in asserting dominance and she wasn't going to be pinned down by a girl half her age.

"What's the real reason you showed me your artwork?" Mrs Brown asked quizzingly. "Come on, I've dealt with thousands of students over the years. I'm experienced with human interaction."

"You don't believe me? I came with good intentions. All I wanted was your insight towards my artwork."

Female intuition kicked in and Mrs Brown knew there was more. Mary's body language had tightened and a few facial expressions had turned the wrong way, however minor.

Mrs Brown sharpened her gaze. "And?"

"And... well... I thought about asking you for a favor."

Now it was the professor's turn to smile. "So the truth comes out. What else did you want from me?"

"I wanted to do a portrait of you. You know, a nude."

Mrs Brown unleashed a powerful laugh. "Ha! Now that was a joke, right? Please tell me you're joking."

"Nope."

Mary shook her head and there was sincerity in her eyes and voice. Their eyes were locked and Mrs Brown could swear she knew what her student was thinking.

"You really mean that?" Professor Brown asked for confirmation.

"Yeah, why not? I think you have an ideal figure"

"No, oh no, you wouldn't want to paint me."

"But why?"

Mrs Brown shook her head. "Why paint me when you have a plethora of beautiful bodies to work with?"

"Because, look at you."

"Hardly a ringing endorsement," the professor said with a feigned smile.

Mary reached out and tucked Mrs Brown's hair behind her ear. It was an inappropriate thing to do with a teacher roughly twice your age, but in the circumstance, formalities could be ignored. Couldn't they?

"Okay, I admire your intelligence. And your elegance. You exude those things in a way that other nude models on campus can't."

"That's very flattering," Mrs Brown replied.

"It's also the truth. So, how about it?"

"I'm flattered, but no."

Mary gave an unsurprising node. "Figured, but it was worth a shot." A moment lingered between them. They both knew what it was. Mary was probably disappointed in the answer, but knew it was the likely outcome. And the professor? Well, she had other ideas.

"Look, I won't pose for you, but I'd love to be a technical advisor of sorts."

Mary's eyebrows lifted. "Technical advisor, eh?"

"Yes. I could give tips, advice, pointers. That sort of thing. I don't claim to be any sort of expert in making art, but I can provide whatever knowledge I have over years of teaching."

"Will you help with my next set of artworks?" Mary asked. "We could meet in a campus art room when no one is there."

"Sure, I can do that. I'd love to assist in any way possible."

"Fair warning though. My preference is in making nudes."

Mrs Brown took a short breath. "I've noticed that."

"I don't know," Mary shrugged. "I'm weird."

"There's nothing weird about the human body."

"True, but I like to venture off into sexuality," Mary replied. "Have you noticed that about my artwork?"

"A bit, yes."

"The more explicit ones I try to sell. I display the tamer ones for school."

The professor tried to hide her surprise. "Oh..."

"Don't worry," Mary laughed. "It's not like porn or anything. It's just that there's more of an emphasis on adult feelings. It's sort of like what you saw a while ago, where my breasts were showing."

"Speaking of which, how do you make a portrait of your own breasts like that? Do you base it on memory?"

"Promise you won't laugh?"

"Swear," the professor nodded.

"I kind of cheat a little bit. I set up a camera on a timer, strike a pose, and then I paint the picture. That's how I get a sexy shot of my breasts when I'm alone."

"That's actually pretty clever."

Mary nodded. "I know, but I won't have to rely on the camera timer anymore now that you're assisting me."

"What do you mean?"

"You can take pictures of me. It'll be fun. Then I'll add a classical European style when I paint whatever images you capture of me."

"Nude?" Mrs Brown asked cautiously.

"Yeah, nudes. Unless of course I've misjudged you, and I'm making a massive fool of myself right now, in which case I'd have to drop your class and hide from you for the rest of my college years. Possibly the rest of my life. So what's it going to be Professor Brown?"

Mrs Brown laughed. "No, you won't need to hide from me, or be embarrassed. Yes, I'll help however I can."

"Awesome. Do you have any experience with nude art? Have you taken any of those classes when you were in college?"

"No and no."

"It's not that big of a deal. Tits are tits. Yours are just as good as mine."

"Not quite," Mrs Brown said, softly shaking her head. "You're 21. I'm turning 43 in a few months. I can assure you, our tits are nothing alike."

"I'll be the judge of that."

There was a wry smile on Mary's face when she said that, and it kind of made Mrs Brown feel...alive.

"I look forward to our meeting, whenever it is," Mrs Brown said. "Text me and we'll work out a time slot."

"A toast; to bare tits."

They picked up their bottles of juice and made a toast, and as they drank, they kept on looking at each other. Mary had that twinkle in her eyes. Mrs Brown felt a longing between her legs.

***

Not long after Mrs Brown arrived home to her apartment that evening, she masturbated. She changed her clothes, rested, and slid a hand underneath her panties as she watched the news.

Her back slouched and curved into the couch. Typically she wouldn't be caught dead in public with poor posture like this. But this was a notable exception. No one was around except for the cable news pundits on the screen.

She heard what they were saying and her eyes were watching the screen, but Mary was on her mind.

There were the usual go-to fantasies that Mrs Brown had. Either she'd seduce a student. Or a student would seduce her. Sometimes this would happen when they were alone in a classroom or her office. Other times it was at her apartment or some place generic.

New ideas were on her mind this time. She imagined herself alone with her beautiful young student in the art room. Mary was striking a pose, just like she did in the painting with her breasts proudly thrust outwards. She imagined herself on her knees, in between Mary's legs.

It was a delicious fantasy that made her ignore the news all together and cum. Her feet curled on the floor. Then she relaxed. A smile formed on her face.

When she'd recovered, she felt a pang of guilt, but the remorse quickly disappeared. It always did. Who would ever find out? Unless of course, Mrs Brown would actually admit her feelings to someone...

***

After several back-and-forth texts, they agreed to meet on Monday near the evening. It was the day where the professor had a late afternoon class and the art studio would have more privacy. The sun would also be going down, creating an interesting shade on the pose, thanks to the large windows on the room.

# CHAPTER FOUR

Professor Brown headed to the Creative Arts building with her things in hand. She was dressed professionally as always, but her clothes and hair looked a little rustled from the busy day.

When she entered the room, her pretty student was already there, barefoot and sitting relaxed on a chair. Mary had pulled her hair back in a loose ponytail and was wearing -- surprisingly --- nothing but a robe.

"Can you close the door?" Mary asked. "I don't want anyone outside to see me. Thanks."

Professor Brown closed the door and looked around, noticing a camera and some art supplies on a nearby table.

"Looks like you're all prepared."

Mary stood, smiling. "Yeah, I was here for like an hour doing a bunch of stuff. Plus, we'd better get this done before anyone walks in."

"Is that likely?"

"At this hour, probably not. But you never know."

"So if anyone did walk in, they'd see you...like this...?"

Mary shrugged. "It would only be someone from the Art Club. In which case, that person would have seen me nude already. We'll also have privacy curtains up anyway, just in case."

"Sounds like a plan."

"You bet."

The professor stepped closer to the table which had all the supplies, while Mary pulled a curtain hanging from a ceiling track around their perimeter.

"Do you know how to use a DSLR camera?" Mary asked.

Mrs Brown picked up the device in question. "In my day, all we had were cameras like this, except they weren't nearly as high-tech. So yes, I know what to do."

"Ready?"

Mary's voice seemed to have a particularly seductive tone.

"I'm ready," Mrs Brown nodded.

The beautiful student untied the belt holding her robe closed, shrugged off the cover, and tossed it aside. She put her hands on her hips and stood there completely naked. It was obvious she was confident in her own skin. She had probably done this countless times in front of numerous people, possibly for hours on end.

She had the physique of an average college girl with a slender waist and curves in all the right places. Though she had defined hips, Mary was small on top. And she was clean-shaven between her thighs.

Mrs Brown's eyes kept going back to those nipples. They were small and pink, just as depicted in the paintings. They hardened as she studied them. But was it from exposure to the cool air...or arousal?

All Mrs Brown knew was that it was in her best interest not to let her own arousal show. After all, she was a teaching professional. Having inappropriate contact with a student was strictly against the rules.

"Well?" Mary asked with her hands up now.

Mrs Brown quietly gulped. "Yes?"

"You're the photographer. Tell me what to do."

"Of course," Mrs Brown said, looking around their confined space. "Well, many classical paintings feature women laying on their sides. So, pick whichever piece of furniture you find most comfortable."

Mary looked to her left and pointed at a black, leather lounge chair. "That one."

It was like something therapists used in all the movies. Long and narrow, it was slightly-scuffed in sections, but it still appeared to have plenty of cushioning.

Mrs Brown approved. "Nice choice."

Her eyes, for whatever reason, ventured to Mary's bare feet as it made smacking noises on the hard floor. Then the student paused before sitting.

"How adult do you want to make this?" Mary asked quizzingly.

Mrs Brown blinked rapidly. "What do you mean?"

"I mean, do you want to make this plain? Or do you want to, you know, push boundaries a little."

"Look, it's against my ethical guidelines to assist you any further, because I know what you're talking about. What we're doing now is already pushing the boundaries. Having said that, it's your artwork. I can't stop you. And we're in private."

Mary smiled. "I'll never tell anyone. Will you?"

"Not a chance." Mrs Brown hoped she wasn't blushing, but her cheeks felt warm. Maybe it was just hot in there?

"Then what's the problem?"

Mary flashed her cute, round ass when she suddenly took a detour to where her backpack lay on another chair. She dug inside for a moment. Then she turned back.

The professor saw that the student had something small in each hand. While she had a strange feeling she knew what they were, she didn't want to believe it. It couldn't be, could it?

"What do you have there?" Mrs Brown gulped, uncertain if she wanted to know the truth.

Mary held it up. "This is my secret weapon when it comes to creating art."

"Is it what I think it is?"

Mary nodded with a wicked expression on her face. "Yep. A vibrator."

"And in your other hand?"

"It's a remote control. For you."

Mary handed the teacher a small device and she took it. It was a slender, palm sized object which had two arrows on it.

"I'm technologically illiterate when it comes to sex toys," Mrs Brown admitted, almost proudly.

"What you're holding is a remote control to my vibrator. Press up to increase the vibrations. Press down to decrease it."

# CHAPTER FIVE

A warm feeling came over Mrs Brown as she now held the power, literally, to control Mary's sexuality. The idea thrilled and surprised her. It was a fantasy the teacher never knew she had, or wanted, until now. But professional conduct was something she took extremely seriously.

"Are you sure about this?" Mrs Brown wanted to confirm. "This seems a bit overreaching for campus activities."

"Are you going to tell anyone?"

"No."

"Then fuck it," Mary winked. "Our secret."

She plopped down on the chair with such force that it scooted backwards and her skin squeaked against the leather seat. Then Mary spread her legs wide.

Mrs Brown stifled a gasp. She could see her student's bared pussy. Even the small vaginal opening between those small lips. She wondered how tight Mary was. But she was not mistaken about the fact that Mary's labia was glistening. The younger woman was definitely aroused.

Next, the student inserted the smooth sex device inside of her little hole, gently pushing it so that it went all the way in. When it was inside, she smiled and looked at her teacher.

"You're the boss," Mary said. "Tell me what to do. How to pose. You control how much it vibrates. Own me."

Mrs Brown naturally thought naughty thoughts. Terrible thoughts. What she so desperately wanted to make Mary do... or do to her. But those were fantasies for later. She had to maintain composure for the sake of her job and ethics.

"Lean to your left," Mrs Brown said.

Mary obeyed. Then the professor raised the camera and aimed the lens, ready to snap a shot.

"Aren't you forgetting something?" Mary asked.

"What?"

Mary feigned clearing her throat and pointed to her own exposed pussy. "The adult nature of our artistic expression."

"It must have slipped my mind."

"You seem nervous?"

The professor looked amused. "I wouldn't say that. I've just never done this before. There's a first time for everything though."

Mrs Brown pressed a button once and it immediately made Mary's knees bend. There was also a small vibrating sound emanating from between the student's legs.

"Mmm...." the student moaned, digging further back into the chair.

"I can already see the difference."

Mary smiled and briefly rubbed her chest. "My nipples are so much harder. They've always been really sensitive."

More delicious and naughty thoughts swirled through Mrs Brown's mind. She tried to push them way, but to no avail.

"I admire your confidence," the teacher said. "You look stunning."

Mary lifted her arms and draped them over the top of the lounge seat. The position stretched her upper body, making her hard nipples even more prominent. Her legs opened even wider, letting that low vibrating sound escape from her pussy.

"I still wish I could be taking pictures of you instead. That would be so much better."

"Why?" Mrs Brown asked, surprised that Mary continued to ride the topic.

"Turn the vibration a little higher and I'll tell you."

There was a sensual sound in Mary's voice, which almost sounded threatening in an erotic way. Mrs Brown felt wetness between her own legs, and she pushed the button to make the vibrator buzz a notch higher.

"Okay," the teacher said.

Mary closed her eyes for a moment to savor the feeling. "I had a fling with a woman your age before."

The revelation made Mrs Brown's toes curl inside her shoes and her breath shorten.

"Really?"

"Yes, really," Mary replied, looking her professor straight in the eyes. "It happened last summer when I worked a part-time job at a clothing boutique. I used to wake up early and help stock the shelves before the place would open. Some days it was just me and the boss in the backroom. She was a little older than you. Before you know it, things happened."

"Like what?"

"Kissing. Touching. Licking. That was my first foray into the world of older women. Not to be crude, but it was a complete game changer in terms of my sexuality."

Mrs Brown gulped. "So it just happened? Seems odd."

"What are you saying? That someone had to be the pursuer?"

Mrs Brown silently nodded.

"That would be me. What? Don't look so surprised. You asked."

An undeniable tension came between them and Mrs Brown's heart raced. She stood there like a fool with the camera and remote control in her hands.

"I'll only take one picture," the professor said. "Then we're done."

"In that case, make it count. Turn the device up another notch. Don't worry. I'm not as innocent as I look, professor. I won't break."

Mrs Brown pushed the button twice. Once, because Mary asked her to. The second time was just to see what would happen. That one caused quite a reaction.

Instantly, Mary closed her eyes and squirmed on the lounge seat. She looked beautiful with her naked body writhing, her legs rubbing together sensually.

But all good things must come to an end. Mrs Brown focused the camera to capture Mary's feet, legs, hips, and breasts. Then snapped a single picture.

"We're done," Mrs Brown said, setting the camera back on the table and pressed the down arrow on the remote to power down the vibrator.

Mary opened her eyes, looking totally unsatisfied. "I almost came, you know."

"You can finish that up yourself. Look, I really should be going. I appreciate you letting me help with your projects. If you need any advice, I'd still love to help, but only through email."

Mary sat upright and clenched her legs shut. "Did I do something wrong? I mean, are you mad at me?"

"You're a wonderful person, Mary, but this is a line I can't cross. I'm sorry. I'll see you in class tomorrow."

Professor Brown did her best to be polite about rejecting the student's advances, and she gave a curt smile and left.

***

The art exhibit was as Mrs Brown had expected. It was an event held in the evening in the Creative Arts building. Most of the attendees were students, the rest were parents, professors, and others in the art community.

Like most, Mrs Brown made an effort to dress nicely, wearing a black dress and heels, along with a purse over her shoulder. Not too fancy. Not too casual. She had spent the better part of half-an-hour mingling with fellow faculty and some of her students, before she was able to explore the collection.

After admiring several, she finally reached Mary's small display. The display as a whole impressed her.

What grabbed Mrs Brown's attention most was the painting showcased in the center of the display. Breasts. Bare breasts. Mary's breasts. It almost made Mrs Brown feel proud that she had helped create this portrait by taking the initial picture. She definitely felt aroused seeing those wonderfully shaped tits once again.

It wasn't like Mrs Brown forgot about that fateful day, either. Since seeing Mary nude, a marathon masturbation session had occurred for the rest of that week. She must have set a new record for herself when it came to finding pleasure with the mental images of a student. Twice a day, she'd touched herself while thinking about Mary in that naked pose. And in each instance, Mrs Brown had imagined herself eating pussy for the first time, or being orally pleasured by the pretty student.

"You have that look again," a female voice said from behind.

Mrs Brown snapped out of her daydream and turned to see Mary standing there, also appropriately dressed for the occasion. Her student, wore a yellow sundress with her hair tied in a ponytail. The girl looked cute. Nothing like the seducer of mature women Mrs Brown found she could be behind closed doors.

"And what look are you referring to?" the professor asked, playing dumb and hoping the subject would change.

"I think you know. It's the same look you always have whenever you see my..."

"Wonderful selection," Mrs Brown cut in. "You're so talented."

"Thanks." Mary lowered her voice when she added, "You're right, it's too public here to talk about that. I want to show you something."

"Oh?"

"I bought you a present to show my gratitude. Come on, in the other room."

They snuck off after checking that everyone else was too busy socializing and having a good time to notice them leaving together.

As they headed down the hall, Mrs Brown found herself hoping they'd go someplace special. When they went up the flight of stairs and into the same art room where Mrs Brown had photographed Mary, her heart jump for joy. Outwardly, she tried to maintain a professional composure.

They entered the unlocked room. This time, both of them entered wearing nice dresses and their hair and makeup done.

"Now for your gift," Mary said, heading over to the drawer where she pulled out a box.

Opening it, Mrs Brown saw it was the exact same model Mary had previously used inside her vagina.

"You're kidding?" Mrs Brown laughed.

"Nope. I bought this for you. A token of my gratitude."

"I can't accept this."

"Why not?"

Mrs Brown tensed, waving her hand at the box. "Because. Well. Look at it."

"I already know what it looks like. You had a good look at it too when it was in my pussy."

"That's not a fair comment."

"Why not?"

"I was helping you," Mrs Brown mumbled. "You make it sound like I was intentionally looking."

Mary took a calmer approach. "Let's face it, you're twice my age. You have way more life experience than I do. But when it comes to sex, you're a student compared to me."

"Is that so?"

"Yes."

Mrs Brown put her hands on her hips. "And how exactly would you know that?"

"Answer this," Mary smirked. "Have you ever slept with another woman before?"

"I won't answer that. Totally inappropriate."

"Well then, I guess I'll have to interrogate you."

Mrs Brown burst out laughing. "This, I'd love to see."

"Hardball then. I like it."

Mary pulled the curtains along the ceiling track, blocking them off from the door. Then Mary stepped towards the professor with a strong sense of purpose, so that they were face to face. There was fierceness in Mary's facial expression and demeanor. This girl was all business.

Mrs Brown gulped. This encounter had been planned. She was sure of it.

Without asking for permission, Mary yanked the front of Mrs Brown's skirt up.

Mrs Brown jolted and tried to push her dress back down, but the younger woman was relentless. Mary tightened her grip on the hem, ensuring that Mrs Brown couldn't lower the material or move away. Then she tugged the black panties to the side, exposing Mrs Brown's pussy before pressing the tip of the small vibrator against her bare skin.

The teacher couldn't move, but she wasn't sure if it was from fear or anticipation of the pleasure she may experience at the hands of her student. Inch by inch, Mary pushed that vibrator up Mrs Brown's cunt, and she just accepted it.

Through it all, their eyes remained locked.

"Don't fuck with me," Mary threatened in the most erotic of ways.

Mrs Brown surrendered. "You have my undivided attention."

"Not yet."

There was a sly grin on Mary's face as she held up the remote control. Suddenly, Mrs Brown's body went stiff, and she heard (as well as felt) the vibrations emanating from below. Swallowing heavily, she wondered how many times Mary had pressed the up arrow button.

"Now answer me," Mary said. "Have you ever fucked another girl? Have you eaten pussy?"

"No."

"But you've thought about it, haven't you?"

"Mary, you're going too far. We have to stop."

"Are you refusing to answer?" Mary asked.

Mrs Brown licked her lips but said, "Yes, I'm refusing."

"You know, Wonder Woman has the Lasso of Truth, I have this," Mary said, holding up the remote control. Slowly and intentionally so that Mrs Brown could see, she pressed her thumb down on one of the buttons. Twice.

"Like I said, don't fuck with me, professor."

Mrs Brown couldn't help closing her eyes and tilting her head back, moaning softly. Her knees threatened to buckle, but she forced herself to stay upright. She focused on clenching her purse in both hands to keep her composure.

"I have..." the teacher moaned.

"You have, what?"

"Thought about it. I've thought about it."

"Figured. You see, I'm good at this."

Mrs Brown licked her lips. "I know."

"I had a feeling from the moment you saw my first nude portrait. It all became clearer after that. When I got naked in front of you? I knew it was only a matter of time before you'd be mine. Admit it, Professor Brown, you have a thing for your students."

# CHAPTER SIX

The big secret. Mrs Brown refused to answer. But Mary -- the girl who shouldn't be fucked with -- seemed determined to pry the answer out of her because the vibrations intensified. Mrs Brown's butt cheeks clenched and her feet rose up so she was standing on her toes.

She could barely whisper as her pussy buzzed. "It's a fantasy of mine."

Mary grinned. "A fantasy that should remain a fantasy? Or a fantasy you'd like to become reality?"

"It should stay a fantasy," Mrs Brown gulped.

"Why?"

Mrs Brown felt like a hostage at that point, but a willing one at that. Of course, she could have left. She could have pulled that vibrator out of her pussy and thrown it on the floor. But her body wouldn't let her move.

And then she answered the question. "My job. My ethics."

"And if no one would ever know?"

"I...I..."

Mary raised her hand to show the remote control. "Answer me, or I'll crank this thing so high, your pussy would feel like it's been buzzed in half."

"...Yes... if it stays a secret."

The words came out almost breathlessly as Mrs Brown admitted her secret fantasy. Although she didn't verbalize all of her wants and desires, she was certain that her emotions were enough to convey the message to a girl as sophisticated as Mary.

And it proved true. There was a twinkle in the girl's eyes.

"Did you pleasure yourself a lot after seeing me naked?"

"Yes."

Mary licked her lips. "What did you think about?"

"Eating your pussy. I had a clear view of it when your legs were spread."

"The good news is, Professor Brown, we're alone now."

"Please, don't..."

Mary put her index finger on the teacher's lips. "Shhh.... Our secret. I'm good at secrets."

"What if anyone comes in here?"

"What do you think the curtains are for?"

Mary took three steps back and laid on the black leather lounge chair. The same chair she had posed naked on before. Except this time, she wore a nice dress. She hiked the skirt up to expose her panties, and she slowly removed them.

Meanwhile, Mrs Brown stood frozen like an utter fool while her pussy continued to buzz.

"Are you coming here?" Mary asked, patting her now bared thigh. "Or do I have to make myself cum?"

"No, you don't."

# CHAPTER SEVEN

"I guess that means you'll be the one making me cum. On your knees. I'll show you how it's done. It's easy once you get the hang of it."

Mrs Brown took a big deep breath and placed her purse down on the table. Then she got on her knees, in front of her new favorite student. Once in position, she got the perfect view of Mary's pussy. It looked freshly shaven. Was it her normal habit, or had it been done in anticipation of this event and the possibilities with her professor?

As Mary spread her legs wider, her thin labia also parted, revealing a glimpse of the glistening pink walls of her vagina. Her clitoris was hard, poking out of its hood. It was inviting, begging to be licked.

Mary seemed to purr when she said, "Start with kisses around my mound."

Mrs Brown obliged and pressed her lips against the smooth, soft flesh. Light kisses at first. Then she kissed harder as her confidence grew. She savored the feeling of her student's skin against her lips. She swore she could almost smell the aroma coming from Mary's aroused pussy. It made her a little dizzy.

"Lick my clitoris," Mary instructed next. "As you must know, different women have different pleasure spots. Some women can cum from their labia being sucked. Others need penetration. Personally, for something like this, I prefer swirls of a tongue around my clit. Orbit around it until you think I'm ready, then put your tongue on it. Now."

An overwhelming feeling came over the professor. The buzzing in her vagina had continued for several minutes now and it felt like she was nearly ready to burst. But she didn't want to disappoint her student, or abandon her fantasy.

So she stuck her tongue out and touched another woman's privates for the first time in her life. Her tongue made swirling motions around her student's stiff clit. It was easy and she felt the warmth of pussy against her face. Whatever she was doing must have been right because it made Mary groan.

"Taste me," Mary said. "Go ahead. Put your tongue inside. I'm sure you've tasted your own juices before. Don't be shy tasting mine. I taste really good. You'll see."

Mrs Brown eagerly moved her tongue lower and used it to press deeper inside of Mary's pussy. She tasted fluid, which was actually quite good. It was runny but with a slightly thick consistency. Like nectar. Natural, sweet, arousing. She pressed her lips around the labia and sucked with her tongue inside, causing Mary to groan with her eyes rolled back.

The door suddenly opened. Thinking fast, Mary turned off the vibrator with the remote control, and both of them froze. The professor looked especially mortified, wondering if her career would be over soon. Thank God for the curtains which protected them.

"Mary, are you in here?" a girl asked.

"Yeah! I'm... ummm... I'm cleaning my clothes!"

"Really?"

"I accidentally pissed in my panties," Mary replied, before cringing to herself because of the horrible excuse.

"You did?" the girl asked, laughing.

"Someone told a really funny joke and it just came out. I'm cleaning my panties as we speak."

"Why aren't you using the bathroom?"

"More privacy here," Mary countered. "Or so I thought. I'll see you down there in a few minutes."

"Okay. We need you in about 10 minutes. Don't rush. There's nothing worse than walking around with wet panties. Trust me, I know all about it. So get that cleaned up. See you then."

If she only knew...

For nearly a minute, the girl remained in the art room to grab some things. Mary pointed to her pussy, silently instructing the professor to keep licking. Mrs Brown did so with the utmost discretion as the unknown girl was still there.

Finally, they heard the door open and close.

"She's gone," Mary told the relieved professor. "Back to work, harder now. I'm almost there. Start sucking again."

Mrs Brown returned to sucking and slurping. The sounds were louder now-- lewd even. Then she heard herself growl as the vibrations started again within her. The pulsing wasn't as intense as it had been before the girl had interrupted them, but it was a steady rhythm that made Mrs Brown's back straighten.

Both of them were in a state of heightened sexual arousal. Not only from the physical pleasure they were giving each other, but also the intense taboo of where they were doing this. Not to mention their respective roles as teacher and student.

"Fuck," Mary moaned. "Fuck, fuck, fuck. Put your tongue all the way inside. Don't pull out. I'm going to fucking squirt in your mouth."

What a shock. Mrs Brown's eyes widened for a moment. What Mary said sounded kind of gross... but also really exciting in a deviant way. The idea of that happening in her mouth from a beautiful student was an opportunity she simply couldn't pass up. She shoved her tongue all the way inside and held it there, with her lips pressed tightly against the labia so nothing would leak.

When Mary reached down to rub her own clit, that was it. She came.

Mary's body suddenly clenched and her head snapped back, eyes closing, legs clenching. A stream of liquid rushed over Mrs Brown's tongue and down her throat. It came in several gushes, then in trickles as it slowed down.

Finally, Mary relaxed and she looked down at her professor with a satisfied grin.

"And that, Professor Brown, is how you eat pussy. It's your turn to cum now. We have an event to return to."

The vibrator was suddenly cranked up higher. Mrs Brown threw her head back and rocked on her knees in front of Mary's wet, glistening pussy. After another couple of minutes, she had to lean her head against Mary's thigh. She needed more. The vibrator wasn't enough. And if they didn't hurry, that girl could come back. She'd only given Mary ten minutes. So Mrs Brown reached down between her own legs now and rubbed her clit in a rapid, circular motion to help herself cum.

She wasn't a squirter by any means, but fluids ran over her fingers and down her thighs. Her gasps came in the form of several quick, panting noises. It sort of pained her that a student of hers was seeing her this way. But then again, they both came in front of each other, and there was nothing to be embarrassed about.

As her orgasm waned, she felt the device turn off and she sighed, silently thanking Mary for her mercy. Mrs Brown quickly tried to compose herself, though she sat on the floor, her dress bunched up around her hips. She couldn't help the giggle when she thought of the irony that she probably needed to clean her dress before heading back to the art exhibition.

"Wasn't that cool?" Mary asked, kissing the top of Mrs Brown's hair. "I was your teacher this time. You were my student."

Mrs Brown kissed Mary's high, then stood up. "I can't deny that, and it was a wonderful lesson."

After removing the vibrator, Mary unexpectedly bent forward, kissing and licking Mrs Brown's wet pussy. Giving her a taste of what a female mouth would feel like against her sex. It was exquisite. When her student slipped her tongue inside, Mrs Brown knew that she was officially a changed woman.

Mary pulled her mouth away. Keeping her eyes on her teacher's, she slowly sucked the small but powerful device clean.

"You're the teacher in class," she said with seductive eyes. "But I'm the teacher when it comes to pussy."

Mrs Brown smiled wide. "Professor Peter, Doctorate of Female Pleasures. I like the sound of that."

"So do I."

Mary stood and they kissed on the mouth. While their tongues played, Mary reached down and fixed Mrs Brown's panties, patted the dress so that it would be nice and neat, and swatted the dust away from the dress after having sat on the floor.

Mrs Brown wrapped the vibrator in several layers of tissue and put it in her purse. After touching up their makeup, it was time for them to head back to the art exhibition.

# THE END

Thank you again for purchasing this book, I hope you have enjoyed it!

**AUTHOR NAME IS ALICIA CASTELLE.**

Could I ask you a favor? If you did enjoy this book, could leave me a review on Amazon? If you search for my name and the title on Amazon you will find it. Thank you so much, it is very much appreciated!

www.ingramcontent.com/pod-product-compliance
Lightning Source LLC
LaVergne TN
LVHW040244140426
836227LV00040B/863